SCAVENGER HUNT HEIST

Don't miss any of the cases in the Hardy Boys Clue Book series!

HARDY BOYS

→ Clue Book ←

SCAVENGER HUNT HEIST

BY FRANKLIN W. DIXON ⇆ ILLUSTRATED BY MATT DAVID

ALADDIN

NEW YORK   LONDON   TORONTO   SYDNEY   NEW DELHI

ALADDIN

An imprint of Simon & Schuster Children's Publishing Division
1230 Avenue of the Americas, New York, NY 10020
First Aladdin paperback edition April 2017
Text copyright © 2017 by Simon & Schuster, Inc.
Illustrations copyright © 2017 by Matt David
Also available in an Aladdin hardcover edition.
All rights reserved, including the right of reproduction in whole or in part in any form.
ALADDIN and related logo are registered trademarks of Simon & Schuster, Inc.
THE HARDY BOYS and colophons are registered trademarks of Simon & Schuster, Inc.
HARDY BOYS CLUE BOOK and colophons are trademarks of Simon & Schuster, Inc.
For information about special discounts for bulk purchases, please contact
Simon & Schuster Special Sales at 1-866-506-1949 or business@simonandschuster.com.
The Simon & Schuster Speakers Bureau can bring authors to your live event.
For more information or to book an event contact the Simon & Schuster Speakers Bureau
at 1-866-248-3049 or visit our website at www.simonspeakers.com.
Book designed by Karina Granda
The text of this book was set in Adobe Garamond Pro.
Manufactured in the United States of America 0419 OFF
4 6 8 10 9 7 5
Library of Congress Control Number 2016954902
ISBN 978-1-4814-8517-3 (hc)
ISBN 978-1-4814-8516-6 (pbk)
ISBN 978-1-4814-8518-0 (eBook)

CONTENTS

Chapter 1

FOFT

"Rawwwr!"

Frank Hardy jumped nearly a foot in the air, splashing the milk from his cereal bowl all over his brand-new navy-blue T-shirt. "Joe! That's not funny!"

"It's not?" Eight-year-old Joe Hardy disagreed. In fact, he was laughing so hard, he thought orange juice would come out his nose. "Don't worry, Frank. I know I do a killer bear impression, but it's just me."

He laughed some more while his brother grumbled under his breath.

"Joe Hardy!"

Joe's laughter died in his throat as soon as he heard his father, Fenton Hardy, shout his name.

"Stop teasing your brother," Mr. Hardy said, peering at Joe over his newspaper. But Joe thought he saw a smile in his father's eyes.

Frank refilled his bowl of Healthy Nut Crunch with fresh milk and took a seat back at the breakfast table with Joe and Mr. Hardy.

"I'm not teasing Frank," explained Joe, slurping the sweet milk from his bowl of Sugar-O's. "I'm helping him face his fears."

"I'm not afraid!" said Frank. But when he looked at his watch and saw that he would be at Bayport Bear Park, along with the other third and fourth graders, in less than an hour, he shivered.

In his nine years, Frank had faced a lot of fears solving mysteries with his younger brother, Joe, and their friends—their dad had even built them a tree house, which served as their official mystery-solving headquarters. But so far, Frank had never faced an actual bear—and he'd hoped he never would. He'd seen a show about bears on TV last year. They were huge, and could smell people, animals, and food from miles away! Not to mention that when they defended themselves, they stood on their back legs and their fur puffed out so they could look extra big!

Suddenly Frank felt a little queasy. "Dad," he moaned, cradling his stomach with one hand. "I don't feel so good."

"No?" Mr. Hardy said. "What's wrong, Frank?"

"He's got FOFT," said Joe, rolling his eyes.

"FOFT?" asked Mr. Hardy.

"Fear of Field Trip," Joe said, cracking a smile in his brother's direction.

"Not that Frank *is* afraid," said Mrs. Hardy, entering the kitchen. "But you two know that you won't have to see any real bears at Bear Park, right? It's just a silly name." She kissed Frank on the top of his head and handed him a fresh T-shirt, which he swapped for his soggy one right at the table.

"Or is it?" Joe waggled his eyebrows up and down dramatically.

Even Frank had to laugh at his brother's ridiculous face this time.

"Dad," Frank said, deciding that it was time for a change of subject. "Do you have any cases for work that you need our help with?"

Fenton Hardy was a private detective, and sometimes he worked with the local Bayport Police Department to help solve crimes. When he needed their help, Mr. Hardy was known to tell Frank and Joe about the cases he worked on; he knew the boys had their own detective club and had solved lots of mysteries of their own.

Mr. Hardy showed his sons the front page of the newspaper he was reading. The headline on the front, in big black letters, read: NY POLICE HUNT FOR JEWEL HEIST ROBBERS!

"A jewel heist!" Joe exclaimed, through a mouthful of Sugar-O's. "Cool!"

"Do you have any leads?" Frank asked seriously.

"A couple," said Mr. Hardy. "While you're on your field trip, I'm going to be at the police station, helping the officers question a suspect."

"Why don't you just arrest him?" asked Joe.

"Because first we have to make sure he committed the crime," said Mr. Hardy. "Remember last year when Joe thought Mrs. Beasley next door stole his bike?"

Frank laughed, his eyes sparkling. "And we found it the next day, in the backyard. Joe forgot he left it there."

"Honest mistake," Joe defended himself. "She was acting suspicious."

"Exactly," said Mr. Hardy. "But if you'd accused

Mrs. Beasley without proof, you'd have looked awfully silly. Same with the jewel heist. Before we arrest someone, we need to have proof he did it, otherwise the real bad guy could get away with robbing that jewelry store."

Frank thought about this for a minute, then took out a pocket notebook that Aunt Trudy had gotten him. Frank and Joe liked to take notes when they were solving a mystery, and this seemed like a very good first note to make in his notebook. *Proof!* he wrote.

"You boys better get a move on," Mrs. Hardy said, pointing at their kitchen clock. "The school bus will be here in ten minutes, and you don't want to miss your field trip."

Frank closed his notebook and placed it in his back pocket. He couldn't help but wonder if missing the field trip was really such a bad thing.

"Watch it, Hardys!" Adam Ackerman, the biggest bully at Bayport Elementary School, pushed past Frank and Joe on his way out of the school bus, stepping on Joe's toes as he went.

They had just arrived at Bayport Bear Park, and Adam was cutting past everyone to make sure he was the first one off the bus.

"Even I waited my turn," Cissy Zermeño told Frank and Joe as they climbed down off the school bus. "And I like to be first and best at everything."

Frank and Joe exchanged a look. No one knew how Cissy liked to be number one better than the Hardys. She always won at everything.

"Okay, everyone," Ms. Potter, one of the chaperones (and a teacher at Bayport Elementary), called out. "Please follow me into the visitors' cabin, single file."

Frank had to admit the park was pretty neat. It was springtime, so everything was green and bright and the birds were singing their chipper songs. After a long winter, it was nice to see leaves on the trees again, and clover-green grass covered the ground. A few picnic tables and grills for cookouts dotted the park. On the outskirts of the property was a thick, sprawling forest with all different kinds of trees.

That must be where the bears live, thought Frank, his heart pounding.

Straight ahead, Ms. Potter led the line of students into a dark-brown log-cabin-type building. In front of it was a wooden sign that said BAYPORT BEAR PARK VISITORS' CABIN.

Inside the cabin, Joe's classmates were crowded around something that he couldn't see.

"Whoa," said Phil Cohen, one of the Hardys' best friends. "Look at that!"

"What is it?" asked Joe, inching toward the center of the crowd.

That was when Frank and Joe saw it—a big yellow ball about the size and shape of a watermelon, covered in bumblebees!

Chapter
2

BEE CAREFUL!

"Get back!" Frank said, holding his hand out in front of his brother for protection. "It's a beehive!"

"You scaredy-cat!" Adam Ackerman taunted, laughing loudly. "It's not a real beehive!"

"Then what is it?" Joe asked, crossing his arms over his chest. Now that he was closer, he could see that the beehive and the bees attached to it were fake—they looked like they were made out of colored paper of some sort. Still, he didn't know what it was or why it was sitting on a table in the middle of the Bayport Bear Park visitors' cabin— and he was pretty sure that Adam didn't, either.

Adam's cheeks reddened. "Why should I tell you what it is?"

Phil Cohen pulled his phone out of his pocket and took a picture, then punched a few buttons. Phil was a tech whiz—he always had the latest electronic gadgets.

"According to my image recognition search," said Phil, "it's a piñata." He pronounced it *pin-ah-ta*.

"*Pin-yah-ta*," corrected Cissy. "My parents get me one every year for my birthday!"

"What's it do?" asked Joe.

"It's filled with toys and candy and stuff! You're supposed to take turns trying to break it open with a baseball bat, and when it all falls out, you get to keep the prizes."

"Did someone say *candy*?" A girl with honey-colored hair and a bubble-gum-pink hoodie spoke up, making a beeline for the piñata.

"I got here first!" Adam shouted, reaching his hand out to grab the piñata.

Fweeeeeeeeeeeet!

The whole class turned toward the sound of someone blowing a whistle.

"Step away from the piñata!" There, standing next to Ms. Potter, was a teenage girl with glossy chestnut hair and a whistle around her neck. She had on a chocolate-brown uniform stitched with green letters that read HEATHER.

"She's a ranger?" Frank asked. "She sure doesn't look like one to me."

Joe shook his head. Heather wore a ranger uniform, but she was also wearing a glittery purple headband, pale-pink nail polish, and hot-pink lip gloss, and she held a cell phone in one hand.

"I'm a junior ranger here at Bear Park," Heather said. "I'll be leading your field trip today."

"But you're a girl," said Adam Ackerman, screwing up his face into a frown.

"I'm a girl who probably knows more about this park and the surrounding woods than a hundred boys put together." Heather stared Adam down. "And *you* should keep your hands off that piñata."

"What's the piñata for?" the girl with the honey-blond hair asked, wide-eyed. "Is it really filled with candy?"

"Who is that?" Joe asked his brother.

"Lolly Sugarman," said Frank. "She's in my class. She's obsessed with candy—I've never seen her without either a lollipop, a chocolate bar, or bubble gum."

"Yes, it's filled with toys and candy. And that's a good question," Heather told Lolly. "Today we're going to divide you all into teams of four. Then you're going to compete . . . in a scavenger hunt!"

There was a murmur among the students, and they immediately began grouping themselves into teams. Frank and Joe called out to their friend Chet Morton, but Heather blew her super-loud whistle and everyone went silent.

"I'll be choosing the teams," Heather said.

"Heather?" said Cissy, her arm raised high in the air. "What's a scavenger hunt?"

"It's a competition," said Heather. "I'm going to be handing out a list of five clues, and each team will have to solve the clues together."

Frank and Joe exchanged excited looks. They were the best at solving clues!

"Then," Heather continued, "you'll have to find and collect the answer to each clue in the park somewhere. For example, a clue might be: What is green with four parts and brings you luck—"

"A four-leaf clover!" shouted Cissy.

"Right." Heather nodded. "So you would have to find a four-leaf clover somewhere in the park. We'll be handing out plastic bags with the clues so you can store your scavenger hunt items as you go."

"How do we know who wins?" asked Cissy.

Heather twirled a lock of hair around her finger. "The winning team is the one that collects all the scavenger hunt items first. Winners get to break open the piñata and divide up the candy and prizes among themselves."

The students began chattering eagerly. Frank was excited about the toy prizes inside, whereas

Joe was more excited about the candy. If they won, they'd know just how to divide up their piñata winnings!

Heather divided everyone up into teams of four. Frank and Joe wound up on the same team, along with Phil Cohen and Lolly Sugarman.

"Okay," Frank said, addressing his teammates. "It looks like our biggest competition will be Cissy Zermeño. Who else is on her team?"

"Oh no," said Joe, glancing at Cissy. "Adam Ackerman is on her team."

"Poor Cissy," said Phil. "Tony Riccio and Seth Darnell are on her team too."

Tony and Seth were both friends of Adam's. They weren't as mean as Adam could be, but they weren't nice like Cissy, either. Joe felt bad for her.

Heather handed each group a set of clues in a sealed envelope, a map of the park, and a bunch of plastic bags and told them not to peek at the clues until she said so. Frank was in charge of holding the envelope for his group.

"We *have* to win," Lolly told her teammates.

"Candy is my number one favorite thing in the whole world!"

Phil looked at her. "You like candy even better than computers?"

"More than *anything*," Cissy said.

"Don't worry," Joe said, grinning. "The Hardy boys are on the case!"

"Okay!" Heather shouted. "It's time to open your—"

Just then the cabin door burst open. And there, standing in the doorway, was the biggest, tallest, scariest bear Frank Hardy had ever seen!

Chapter 3

BEARY SCARY

"*Graaaawwwwwr!*" a rough voice rumbled.

The class screamed.

"It's a fake!" Joe Hardy shouted, stepping forward and pointing at the figure in the doorway.

The class gasped. Frank thought he could feel his heart skip a beat.

The man in the bear suit seemed to be talking now. But all anyone could hear was *mumble, mumble, mumble.* He was still wearing his bear mask.

Heather stared at the man in the bear suit. "Your mask," she prodded, rolling her eyes.

The man laughed and removed the bear mask from his head. "Sorry about that, kids! The young man in the red shirt," he said, indicating Joe, "is right! I'm not a real bear."

"Who are you, then?" Elisa Locke asked, narrowing her eyes.

"My name is Bo Bobbleton," he said, stepping out of the bear costume. Underneath it, he wore a chocolate-brown ranger uniform, just like Heather's. He was tall and muscular, with black hair that was streaked with silver and a stubbly silver beard. Even without the costume, he looked a little bearlike. "But you can call me Ranger Bo!"

"I told you that suit would scare them!" Heather said, slipping her phone into the back pocket of her uniform.

"I wasn't scared!" Joe said. "My mom told me that we wouldn't see any *real* bears at Bear Park."

Bo nodded. "And we'd like to keep it that way, so before you begin your scavenger hunt, I'm going to go over some of our Bear Park rules and regulations. It's for your own safety."

Joe wrinkled his nose. He hated rules!

Frank didn't mind, though. Rules helped everyone stay safe.

"First," said Bo, holding up a finger like he was pointing to the sky, "you must solve the clues with your whole team, or else it doesn't count."

Joe shrugged. That one wasn't so bad.

"Second, no food or drink outside this cabin."

"Why not?" Cissy asked.

Bo and Heather exchanged a look, which made Frank curious. They sure seemed uneasy about something!

"We don't want food being left out and attracting any animals," Ranger Bo explained.

"Like . . . *bears*?" Frank gulped.

"There's no reason to be afraid of the wildlife, but keeping food and drink in the cabin and making sure you observe rule number three will ensure that there are no problems."

Problems? Frank thought. He couldn't help but notice that Ranger Bo hadn't exactly answered no.

"And please don't feed the wildlife, even if they look cute," Heather added.

"What's rule number three?" Joe asked.

"No wandering off the path into the woods," said Ranger Bo.

Once the students agreed to obey the park rules, Ranger Bo counted down from three, and everyone ran outside at once, excited to look at the first clue.

Once their team was outside, Frank opened the envelope and selected a note card with *Clue #1* at the top. He showed Lolly, Joe, and Phil what it said:

Light as a _____
in all kinds of weather.
Birds use me to fly
all through the sky.

"That one's easy!" said Frank, smiling. "The answer is 'feather.'"

"Great job!" said Joe.

"But where do we find one of those?" asked Phil.

"Well," said Lolly, after blowing a huge bubble with her neon-purple bubble gum. "Birds make nests in trees. Maybe we'll find a feather near the woods?"

The team headed for the forest beyond the clearing where the visitors' cabin and picnic tables were.

"Look at this one!" said Joe, running over to a huge oak tree. It had a hole in the center of its trunk shaped like a long oval—almost like a mouth open in a yawn. Next to it was a pretty maple tree with polished-looking reddish-purple leaves.

The group searched beneath the trees. Before long, Joe found a shiny black feather lying on top of the grass under the big oak.

"Congratulations!" boomed a voice just behind them. "You found the first scavenger hunt item!"

Frank and Joe turned to find Ranger Bo beaming at their team.

"You're the first team to find the first item," added Bo.

"One step closer to all that candy," said Lolly, her eyes twinkling.

"That's right, young lady," said Ranger Bo. He walked off toward another team that was farther along the path.

Joe grinned. "We have two amateur detectives on our team," he said. "We're sure to win this thing!"

"Read the next clue, quick!" said Lolly. "I think I just saw Adam Ackerman with a white feather!"

Frank opened a plastic bag, and Joe dropped the feather in. Then Phil produced Clue #2 from the envelope and read it aloud to his team:

> *"You'll find me where pigs roll around,*
> *and where rain meets dirt.*
> *You'll find me on the ground—*
> *just don't get me on your shirt!"*

"Where pigs roll around?" asked Frank.

"Pigs are dirty," said Lolly. "But the answer can't be dirt, because the clue says that it's dirt mixed with rain."

The group thought for a minute.

"Wait," said Phil. "I think I know the answer!"

"You can't look it up on your phone," said Frank. "That's cheating."

"I didn't look it up," Phil said. "But I know that dirt and water make mud—that must be it!"

"Mud?" asked Lolly, sticking out her tongue. "Gross!"

Joe nodded, stifling his laugh—girls were so weird sometimes. "Pigs like to roll around in mud, and I know my aunt Gertrude hates when I get mud on my shirt."

"But where will we find mud around here?" asked Phil, tapping his phone. He looked at the screen and then back to his teammates. "According to the weather forecast, it hasn't rained in over three weeks."

Frank nodded. "And the only way to make mud is with water and dirt."

Joe kicked at the ground, uncovering layer after layer of dry-as-dust dirt. "Nothing," he said. "Does anyone else have any ideas?"

"It wouldn't matter where in the park we went," said Frank, unfolding a map of Bear Park that each team had been given. "If it hasn't rained and there are no lakes or streams—which, according to the map, there aren't—all the dirt would be the same."

Suddenly Lolly gasped. "I've got it!" she exclaimed, taking her backpack off her back and unzipping it.

Joe gave Frank and Phil a quizzical look.

Lolly produced a thermos from her backpack.

"There's mud in your thermos?" asked Phil.

"No, silly!" Lolly's curls dazzled in the sunlight. "My mom and I made SugarSugar Punch last weekend. All we had to do was mix the flavored powder with water."

"What does that have to do with mud?" asked Frank with a serious look on his face.

Lolly unscrewed the top of the thermos and poured the punch on the ground next to the nearby picnic table, on top of a patch of dirt. She used a stick to mix the dirt and the SugarSugar Punch together. The result was a thick brown sludge.

"She made mud!" said Phil.

"Of course!" said Frank. "The SugarSugar Punch is made from water, and water and dirt make mud!"

"Hey, Frank," said Joe. "Think fast!" Quick as lightning, Joe scooped up a handful of mud and flicked it at his brother. It landed on Frank's forehead with a splat.

At first Frank froze. But soon enough he was laughing so hard tears were rolling down his face. He retaliated by throwing a handful of mud at Phil and one at Joe.

Laughing hysterically and not wanting the only girl member of their group to feel left out, Phil smeared some mud on Lolly Sugarman's cheek. She was laughing with the rest of her team, until . . .

"My hoodie!" Lolly hollered.

A quarter-size splotch of sugar-mud had fallen from Lolly's cheek onto her soft pink hoodie.

"I'm sorry, Lolly," said Phil. "It was an accident!"

"My mom's going to be so mad," she said, chin quivering. "This is a brand-new hoodie!"

"Hey, just like the clue said!" laughed Joe.

Lolly glared at him.

"Or not," he said weakly.

Frank tried to reason with her. "Lolly, what if you tried washing it off in the restroom? Our aunt Gertrude takes stains out by running our clothes under the water faucet sometimes."

After a couple more chin quivers from Lolly,

the boys convinced her to go back to the cabin's restroom and try to the get mud out of her hoodie. But after nearly ten minutes, they were starting to get worried. What was taking so long? They wanted to open the next clue, but according to Ranger Bo's scavenger hunt rules, they all had to read and solve the clue together, or it didn't count.

"She's taking forever!" complained Joe. "What, did she fall in?"

Finally Frank, Joe, and Phil decided to follow Lolly into the cabin. After all, the other teams had probably caught up to them, so they couldn't afford to waste more time. "She must be in here somewhere," said Frank, pushing open the door to the visitors' cabin.

But all three of them stopped short, their mouths open wide in shock.

Because there, on the table where the piñata had once sat, were now only a few shreds of yellow paper—the prize piñata was missing!

Chapter 4

A CRIME AGAINST CANDY

"What happened to the candy?" Joe Hardy exclaimed. He and the others ran over to the table.

"Someone stole the piñata!" said Phil. He combed his fingers through the scraps of yellow tissue paper and little pieces that used to be the fake bumble bees attached to the hive. "I wonder what happened?"

Just then Adam Ackerman came from another part of the cabin into the main room. He wore his usual smirk, as well as a ring of dark chocolate smudged all around his lips.

"What did you losers do to my prize?" he asked. Then, upon getting a closer look at the mess on the table, he shouted, "It's gone!"

"As if you didn't know!" said Phil pointedly. "You had your hands on that piñata the second you saw it!"

Adam laughed. "Are you crazy?" he asked. "Does it *look* like I have your stupid beehive?"

"No," admitted Frank. "But it *does* look like you've eaten quite a bit of candy—which is what was *inside* the piñata."

Adam looked genuinely stumped. "I'm sick of your stupid detective club always blaming me for everything," he said.

"If you didn't eat the piñata candy," said Joe, pointing back at the table, "then what's with the chocolate mustache?"

Adam's eyes widened. He wiped his mouth on the back of his hand. "Fine," he said at last. "Ranger Bo caught me eating a chocolate bar while we were out in the woods. He made me come back to the cabin to get rid of it before it attracted any animals."

"It doesn't look like you got rid of it," Frank said, eyeing the chocolate still on Adam's face.

"He said I had to get rid of it," Adam grumbled. "He didn't say that I couldn't get rid of it in my mouth."

The restroom door slammed, and Lolly Sugarman walked out. Her pink sweatshirt still had a brown spot on it, but it was a little faded now. And wet.

"What happened?" She ran to the table and saw the few shreds of confetti, all that remained of the piñata. "My beautiful piñata full of delicious candy!" she moaned.

"Oh boy," said Joe, under his breath. "This isn't going to be pretty."

Phil explained to Lolly what had happened in the past few minutes.

"Did you see anything when you first came in, Lolly?" asked Frank. He pulled the notebook out of his pocket, along with a pen.

Lolly shook her head. "No," she said. "The piñata was still here when I walked in. I remember admiring it." She tightened her grip on her backpack.

Frank and Joe exchanged glances. Lolly was acting sort of strange—like she was uncomfortable about something.

"Was Adam here when you came in?" Joe asked.

"No, no one else was here. I noticed the back door to the cabin was open, so I thought someone might be inside—but when I called out, there was no one there. After that, I closed the door and went into the restroom to try to get the mud out." She frowned at her sweatshirt.

"See?" said Adam, scowling. "I got here five minutes before you three did. You dummies are barking up the wrong tree! Again!"

"I still say Ackerman did it," said Phil. "He's acting suspicious."

Frank looked at the first page of his new detective's notebook. It had only one word written on it, the one he'd written earlier that morning after his dad had told him about that jewel heist.

Proof!

They couldn't accuse Adam of stealing the piñata without better proof.

"Let's think this through," said Frank. "Lolly got here first, which we know because the cabin was empty when she came in. And by the time we came in, Adam was here."

"Duh," said Adam, crossing his arms over his chest.

"The piñata was still here when Lolly went into the restroom," Joe said, picking up where his brother left off. "But when we came into cabin, it was gone. Plus, Adam was here."

"If I stole the piñata," said Adam, "then where is it? And where is the candy?" He pulled his pants pockets inside out, showing everyone they were empty.

"You could have eaten it all," said Phil. "And then thrown away the piñata part."

"No, Adam's right," Lolly sighed. "In my professional candy-eating opinion, five minutes is not enough time for anyone to have eaten a whole piñata full of candy. Not even *me*."

Phil looked disappointed, but he didn't say anything.

"I guess we better tell Ranger Bo," said Frank.

After they told Ranger Bo and Heather what had happened, the two rangers convened the rest of the teams inside the cabin and made an announcement— or tried to. The students were so upset over the missing scavenger hunt prize that groans and whispers

↰ 33

were spreading around the room quickly. Finally Ms. Potter had Heather blow her whistle, and everyone quieted down.

"Everything will go on as scheduled," said Ranger Bo.

"But what will the winner get now that there's no piñata?" asked Cissy.

"The adults will find a new prize while you kids go back to your scavenger hunt," said Bo. He patted his pockets, as though looking for something he couldn't find.

"You gave them to me for safekeeping, remember?" Heather dangled a set of keys in front of Bo's eyes.

He put a palm to his forehead. "I forgot!"

"Why don't you let me go to the store?" said Heather eagerly.

Ranger Bo looked at her like he wanted to say something, but stopped himself. Then he said, "I'll figure something out. You go ahead and help with the scavenger hunt."

"Suit yourself." She shrugged. But Bo was still

looking at her suspiciously when everyone else began looking for clues again.

"Are you thinking what I'm thinking?" Joe asked Frank.

Frank nodded. "It looks like Team Hardy has a new case to solve!"

Chapter 5

SWORD FIGHT!

After the rest of the kids had gone back outside to resume their scavenger hunt, Frank and Joe huddled up. While they huddled up, Heather was off in the corner, typing furiously on her phone.

"Let's try to get the facts down," said Frank, opening his notebook.

Joe nodded. "We've got our *what*. Now we just have to figure out the *who*, *when*, *where*, and *why*."

Frank scribbled the first *W* into their notebook, followed by the rest of the *W*s:

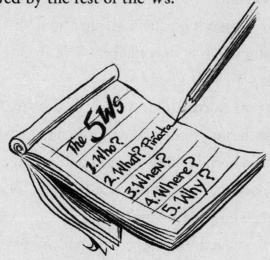

"What are you guys doing?" Lolly asked, leaning over the notebook.

"Solving a mystery," Joe said. "These are the five *W*s." He pointed to the page in front of them. "It's how we solve our cases."

"You mean you've solved mysteries before?" she asked.

"Tons of them!" Phil told her.

"Would you like to help us solve this one?" Frank asked Lolly. "We can use all the help we can get!"

"That sounds like fun . . . ," she said, trailing off. She looked out the window at the other teams, which were hard at work on the scavenger hunt. It looked like Adam, Cissy, Seth, and Tony were already starting their search for Clue #3.

"Are you worried that we'll miss the rest of the scavenger hunt?" Frank asked Lolly. He knew how much she'd been looking forward to the prize candy.

She nodded, looking down at her feet. "Not that it matters who wins anymore."

Frank nudged his brother and put the detective's notebook back in his pocket.

"C'mon," Joe said. "We can do the scavenger hunt and try to solve the mystery at the same time."

"Really?" asked Lolly, her blue eyes brightening.

"Really!" said Frank. "Besides, Ranger Bo said he was getting us a new prize."

"Even if it's not candy." Lolly sighed.

"Who cares?" Phil said. "As long as we beat Adam Ackerman!"

Frank, Joe, Lolly, and Phil went back outside and opened their third clue.

Nearby, Elisa Locke was jumping out of the way while Chet Morton poured his water bottle onto the dirt near her pretty black boots. If they hurried, they could still catch up!

Phil and the others all read the clue:

_____s and stones
will break our bones.
To hit the bull's-eye,
I'm shaped like a Y.

Lolly placed a finger on her chin. "My sister used to say that when I'd call her names."

"What?" Joe asked.

"Sticks and stones will break my bones, but words will never hurt me."

"So we're looking for a stick?" said Phil.

"Not just any stick," whispered Frank. He leaned into his teammates so none of the other teams would hear. "We need to find a Y-shaped stick!"

"Everyone else is in the woods," observed Joe. "Maybe we should look for our stick over there, near the park benches. There are trees over there, too—I'll bet a bunch of sticks have fallen on the ground underneath them."

He pointed toward a circular space in the middle of the park, where a few park benches formed a semicircle. He was right; there were trees all around the benches, shading them from the bright spring sunshine.

When they got there, everyone got down on their hands and knees and started looking for a stick in the shape of a Y.

As they searched, they talked some more about what Joe had named the Case of the Scavenger Hunt Heist, and Frank jotted down notes in his notebook.

"What about the *where*?" Joe asked. "We know that one."

"True," Frank said, winding his way around the dirt path to the woods. "The candy and piñata were taken from the visitors' cabin."

"We can keep looking while you write that down," Lolly offered helpfully.

"Thanks!" Frank said, scribbling in his notebook. While he was writing, he held the paper in place so the balmy spring wind wouldn't turn the page.

Where: Bear Park visitors' cabin

"Now all we need are the *when*, the *why*, and the *who*," he told the others.

"We know the *when*, don't we?" asked Joe. He was on his knees, sifting through a pile of twigs on the ground. Some of them were sort of wavy, but none of them looked exactly like a Y.

"It was after I went inside to get the stain off my shirt," said Lolly.

"And that was at eleven thirty," said Phil. "I remember, because I checked my watch."

Frank wrote *11:30* in his notebook.

"And ten minutes later, we followed her inside," said Phil. He knelt down on the ground and brushed aside some leaves to see if there were any Y-shaped twigs hiding underneath them—no such luck.

"So the piñata had to have been stolen between

eleven thirty and eleven forty," said Frank, making another note.

"That's not very much time," said Joe, dusting some dirt off the knees of his jeans.

"That was a big piñata," Lolly pointed out. "I wonder where it went that fast—and where the candy inside went."

"That's a good point." Frank thought for a minute and looked back at that word he'd written in the notebook earlier that morning—*Proof!* If they found the candy, he bet that they'd find proof of who'd taken the piñata.

"It has to be close by," said Joe. "The thief couldn't have gotten far with it in just ten minutes."

"Got it!" Phil shouted, pointing at a stick under a park bench.

But just as he picked it up, Seth Darnell and Tony Riccio knocked it out of his hands—with their own Y-shaped sticks!

"En garde!" shouted Tony, holding his stick like a sword.

Seth brandished his own stick like a sword too.

"'My name is Inigo Montoya,'" he said, quoting the movie *The Princess Bride*, which had one of Frank and Joe's very favorite sword fights of any movie, ever. "Prepare to—*ahhhhh!*"

Joe came at Seth with a stick he'd broken off a nearby tree, and the two boys toppled to the ground, laughing.

Soon all the boys were having a mock sword fight.

"You guys!" moaned Cissy, standing beside Lolly with her hands folded over her chest. "Stop! We're wasting time!"

"Yeah," added Lolly. "Stop horsing around."

"She's right," said Cissy. "We'll never win if you keep playing sword fight."

Adam charged Frank with his stick, but Frank ducked just in time. Adam ran right into the tree!

He got to his feet quickly, though, just in time to block Frank's swipe.

"Stop!" Cissy repeated. She turned to Lolly. "Boys are so dumb sometimes."

They watched as the boys continued to parry with the Y-shaped sticks.

"What should we do?" Cissy asked.

Lolly took a deep breath, then threw herself into the middle of the boys' imaginary sword fight, holding out her palms as if to say *Stop!*

Phil, who had been running at Joe with his stick-sword, ran right into Lolly, knocking her—and her backpack—to the ground.

The second it hit the ground, Lolly's backpack flew open—and heaps and heaps of candy spilled out like lava out of a volcano.

"Is that . . . ?" Phil blinked at the candy on the ground.

"A piñata's worth of candy!" Frank said.

Chapter

6

OOEY CLUEY

Lolly pushed herself up off the ground. "Now my new sweatshirt has a mud spot *and* a grass stain."

"Lolly," said Joe, eyes widening. "Where did all that candy come from?"

"Isn't it obvious?" Adam snatched the backpack out of Lolly's grasp. "Lolly Sugarman stole the scavenger hunt prize!"

Cissy gasped and ran to Adam's side, her eyes on the backpack.

"Did not!" said Lolly. She grabbed her backpack and began shoveling the spilled candy back inside. Then she paused and looked at her team.

Frank, Joe, and Phil were all gaping at the candy pieces still on the ground. None of them knew what to say—it didn't look good for Lolly.

"You believe me, don't you?" Lolly asked.

"Well . . . ," said Phil, red-faced.

"I mean, why do you have all that candy?" asked Joe.

Lolly rolled her eyes. "Guys, this is my personal candy stash. I always have it on me, at all times."

Cissy looked at her feet. "I don't know. . . ."

Lolly stood. She held a handful of the candy that had spilled out of her backpack. The wrappers were bright purple, with white polka dots. "Do you see what this is?" she asked the boys.

"Proof that Team Hardy won't be winning the scavenger hunt?" Adam asked, cackling at his own joke.

"It's Grapelicious Ooey Gooey gum," said Lolly, as if the answer was obvious.

"So?" Adam asked.

"So, I'm *always* chewing Grapelicious Ooey Gooey gum. Ask anyone!"

"How can we be sure?" asked Phil.

"Because I said so," said Lolly, hugging her bag tight to her chest.

"What else is in that bag?" asked Adam. "More candy?"

"You can't just go accusing me because you don't know who else could have done it," said Lolly. "It's not fair. I was helping with the investigation and everything."

Frank and Joe looked at each other.

"She's right," admitted Frank. "Plus, there's only gum in her bag—and Heather said there were toys and other kinds of candy in the piñata."

"And real detectives have to have a reason to go through people's things—our dad told us," Frank added.

Joe nodded. "It's called 'probably cause.'"

"*Probable* cause," corrected Frank. "And it means we need to leave Lolly alone, unless we have a real reason to believe she stole the candy."

Cissy shrugged. "Lolly *probably* took the candy, *'cause* she loves to eat it so much! She's sugar crazy!"

"But that's also the reason why she could be telling the truth," Frank reasoned. "She loves candy, so it shouldn't be a big surprise that she's carrying a bunch of it around in her bag."

"Okay," said Joe. He faced Lolly—he couldn't help but feel bad for her. "If something else comes up and it looks suspicious for you, though, will you agree to show us everything in your bag?"

Lolly nodded. "I guess."

"Let's go," Adam said to his team. "This is getting boring."

Cissy, Adam, Seth, and Tony stalked off with their Y-shaped sticks. Phil put the stick he'd found before the sword fight into a clue bag. It was time to open the new clue—before Adam's team beat them.

Lolly smiled her thanks at the Hardy boys and offered them, and Phil, a piece of purple gum, which they took and popped in their mouths, competing to see who could blow the biggest bubble.

"Howdy there, kids!" boomed Ranger Bo, coming upon the group. "How's your scavenger hunt going?"

"We're just about to open Clue Number Four," said Phil excitedly.

Ranger Bo patted the pockets of his brown pants, then his jacket pockets, as if he was looking for something. "Clue Number Four?" he asked. "That's my favorite!"

"Really?" asked Phil. "How come?"

"Open it up and find out for yourself!" said Ranger Bo. "I'm off to look for my hat."

With that, Bo walked off, looking under park benches and picnic tables as he went.

"Did anyone else notice his hat was on his head?" asked Phil.

"Me!" chorused Lolly, Frank, and Joe.

"He really is forgetful, isn't he?" said Frank.

The team sat at a wooden picnic table while Joe opened the fourth clue. They leaned in as he read it aloud:

> *"I turn color in fall*
> *but that's not all.*
> *I should have a few holes;*
> *being bug food take its tolls."*

The group thought for a minute.

"I understand the first part," said Frank, running his finger over the grooves in the picnic tabletop. "But not the second."

"What's the first part?" Joe asked.

"Leaves?" said Phil. "Leaves turn colors in the fall."

"Exactly," agreed Frank. "But what's the bug part?"

"Don't bugs eat leaves?" Lolly asked, snapping her purple bubble gum. It was already fading, turning from bright purple to lavender.

Joe nodded. "Yup, they do! And when they eat the leaves . . ."

"They leave holes in the leaf!" said Frank, understanding.

"So we're looking for a bug-eaten leaf with holes in it for proof?" asked Phil.

"That's right," said Frank. "Where should we start?"

"I think it's time to go into the woods," suggested Lolly, rising from her seat. "There are more leaves there than anywhere else in the park."

The boys followed her lead, all the way to the wooded path. They saw a few different teams on their way. Elisa had just found her Y-shaped stick, and Ellie Freeman's team hadn't even managed to make their mud yet!

But Adam's team was still neck and neck with the Hardys' team.

"I think we should look here," said Lolly, stopping in front of a big, leafy elm tree. "This one has a ton of leaves—some of them must have bug holes."

"Good idea," said Frank.

Lolly and Frank focused on the leaves they could reach on the tree, and Phil and Joe knelt down and checked the fallen leaves on the ground.

Frank got on his toes and pulled a leaf off the tree. For the most part, it was smooth and bright green, like the grass. But it had four tiny, pin-size holes in one corner where the edges were browning.

"Got one!" he exclaimed.

But when he turned to look at his team, they were all looking past him, under the tree.

Frank turned to follow their gaze. There, mixed in with the leaves and branches right next to the tree trunk, was a bunch of shredded yellow paper.

"It's from the piñata!" shouted Phil.

Joe picked some shreds up and examined them. He spotted a blur of movement out of the corner of his eye and looked up.

"Look!" Joe said. "Up there!"

TREE HUGGER

There, standing on a thick, sturdy branch just above Frank and Joe Hardy's heads, was Heather.

"Ranger Heather?" said Lolly, her mouth dropping open.

Frank couldn't see what Heather was doing, but he noticed that one of her arms was raised high in the air, as if she was trying to reach something.

Heather lowered her arm, and when she did, Frank and Joe saw that she had her phone in her hand.

"Be right down!" She wrapped her hands around one branch, then another, making her way down from the tree.

By the time Heather finally jumped to the ground, she had a leaf in her perfect hair, and pieces of broken tree bark clung to her ranger uniform.

"I was just trying to get better phone service," she told them.

"In the tree?" Phil asked.

Heather nodded. "This park gets, like, no Wi-Fi."

Phil looked confused. "Of course not," he said. "It's a park!"

Joe leaned in to whisper to his brother. "Do you think she could be a suspect?" he asked.

Frank wasn't sure. It looked suspicious that they'd found Heather so close to pieces of the piñata. But what was her motive for stealing it in the first place? Frank leaned down, picked up the shredded yellow paper bits, and stuck them in one of the clue bags for their scavenger hunt items.

"What's that?" Heather asked, pointing at the pieces of piñata in Frank's bag.

"Evidence," explained Joe.

"Of what?" Heather asked. She plucked a tub of lip gloss from her front pocket and smoothed the sticky, shiny goo over her lips.

"We're investigating the case of the missing scavenger hunt prize," Frank said.

Heather's phone chimed like a bell—it was the same sound Mrs. Hardy's phone made whenever she got a text.

Heather tapped her phone a couple of times, made a few swipes across the screen, and then locked it. She placed the phone back in her pocket and looked up at them.

Joe wondered if she'd really been listening to what his brother had said. "Did you see anyone around here looking like they were up to trouble?" he asked Heather.

"I don't think so," she said. "Why?"

"Because," Frank said, holding up the bagged pieces of piñata, "we found the missing piñata pieces right here under this tree."

Heather raised her eyebrows. "I wonder how those got there."

Joe looked at her warily. "We were hoping you could tell us that."

Heather leaned forward, placing her hands on her knees so that she was closer to Joe's height. "Why?" she asked. "Am I a suspect?" She laughed, throwing her head back a little like it was the funniest thing she'd ever heard.

"We're not ruling anyone out," said Frank carefully. He didn't want to single her out the way Adam had with Lolly earlier, but he didn't want to lie, either.

"I think it's time for you kids to get back to your scavenger hunt," Heather said, looking skeptical. "Ranger Bo just texted me—he's gone out to get the new prize, and I'm in charge while he's gone."

"How come he didn't want you to go?" Phil asked, voicing a question that was in Frank's head.

Back at the visitors' cabin, Heather had seemed to really want to go out to get the new prize herself. Ranger Bo had said no pretty quickly—and Frank and Joe wanted to know why.

Heather twirled her hair around a seashell-pink-painted fingertip. She bit her lip, as though she wanted to say something but wasn't sure if she should.

"Ranger Bo is my dad," Heather said finally. "He

doesn't like me to leave the park during work hours, because he's afraid I'll be on my phone the whole time."

Frank and Joe exchanged a look. Did that count as a motive? If Heather was mad at her dad, maybe she'd have sabotaged the scavenger hunt prize. Or . . .

Far off in the distance, Frank heard a bunch of squeals and shouts. The team jogged down the path and searched the path through the trees to see what was going on.

It was Adam's team!

"We're going to win!" Cissy shouted. She turned to Adam, who was holding a clue envelope. "Just one clue left—hurry up and open it!"

Fweeeeeeet!

Just behind Frank and Joe stood Heather, her whistle still in her mouth.

"Twenty minutes left!" she shouted. "Twenty minutes! Finish

up your last clue and meet back in the visitors' cabin in twenty minutes!"

"Oh no!" said Joe, turning to the team. "Adam's team is beating us, and we haven't even solved the mystery yet. What do we do?"

Lolly held up the final clue. "You help us solve the clue, and Phil and I will go find it while you two work out the mystery. Sound like a plan?"

"Let's do it!" said Joe.

Chapter 8

STAY BACK!

When animals travel,
they leave this mark.
Last clue to unravel
in Bayport Bear Park!

"The note at the bottom of the clue says that we have to take a picture of two different examples, instead of putting whatever it is in a plastic bag," said Phil.

Frank tucked the last clue away in his back pocket. This was the hardest clue yet, but he knew that if they worked together, they could solve it.

"Animals travel?" Lolly asked. "What does that mean?"

"Let's think. How do animals travel?" Frank asked.

"Bunnies hop," suggested Lolly.

"And birds fly," Joe said. "But I don't know what that has to do with the clue." He leaned against the maple tree behind him, causing a squirrel nearby to startle and scamper away. As it ran, the squirrel scattered a spray of dirt and crunched through old fallen leaves.

Frank tiptoed toward the leaves the squirrel had upset. "Wait a minute," he said. "Did you guys see that?"

"What?" asked Phil. "The squirrel?"

Frank knelt down and looked closely at the ground. It was faint, but when he pushed aside the leaves and branches, Frank could see where the squirrel had left an imprint of his paw in the dirt. It looked like a mini

version of a dog's paw print, but with little lines at the ends where the claws were.

"Look!" Frank said, calling them over.

"Is that from the squirrel?" Joe asked, peering at the print in the dirt.

"When it ran, it left its mark!" Phil exclaimed.

"The answer to the clue is animal tracks," said Joe. "So if we take a picture of the squirrel's paw print, that means we're done!"

"Almost," corrected Lolly. She popped another

piece of Ooey Gooey into her mouth and chewed around her words. "It says we have to take a picture of *two* different animal tracks. We only have one."

Phil took out his phone and snapped a picture of the squirrel print. Then he reminded Frank and Joe that he and Lolly would look for the next set of tracks while the Hardys went to work on solving the scavenger hunt heist.

The group went deeper into the woods, making sure to stick to the trails. Around them, they could hear other groups moving around. Chet Morton and Elisa Locke were bagging their bug-eaten leaf to their right, and Ellie Freeman was just reading the last clue aloud to her team.

Joe didn't see Adam or anyone else from Adam's group, so there was no way to know whether they'd already found their first tracks. He pushed the thought out of his mind. It was time to focus on their case!

"Okay," Frank said. "We have fifteen minutes left to solve this case—let's get cracking!"

"I'll set my timer," said Joe.

Frank could feel his heart pounding. He'd never had to solve a case to a timer before, and with so little to go on!

As they walked, Frank pulled out his trusty notebook and showed his brother what they had so far:

> Who: Adam? Lolly? Ranger Heather?
> What: stolen piñata
> When: between 11:30 and 11:40 a.m.
> Where: Bear Park visitors' cabin
> Why: ????

"Let's start with Adam," suggested Frank. "Why would he want to steal the prize?"

Joe shrugged. "Adam doesn't *need* a reason to cause trouble," he said. "He just does!"

"True," Frank said, sidestepping a fallen tree branch. "What about . . ." He lowered his voice. "Lolly?"

"I heard that!" Lolly called from ahead, glancing at the Hardys.

Frank felt bad, but Lolly was smiling, which

made him feel a bit better. Joe and Frank walked fast to catch up with Lolly and Phil.

"My motive is simple," Lolly added, surprising the two brothers. "Everyone knows how much I love candy!"

"Um, that's true," said Frank, making a note next to her name.

"What's Heather's motive, then?" asked Joe.

"She could have done it because she was mad at her dad," said Frank, making another note. "Maybe she wanted to get back at him for not letting her be on her phone?"

"You guys might be great detectives," Lolly said, ducking under a low-hanging branch. "But you don't know anything about girls!"

"I think I see something up there," Phil said. He pointed toward where the path broke off in two different directions. He jogged ahead.

"What do you mean, Lolly?" asked Frank.

"Heather was awfully quick to volunteer to run out and get a new prize after we discovered the original one had been stolen," Lolly added.

"You think she could have stolen the prize just for the excuse to leave and get a new one?" Frank asked.

Lolly nodded. "That way, she could be on her phone all she wanted!"

Up ahead, Phil had stopped at the fork in the path and was pulling out his phone.

"Did you find something?" Joe called out, running to look over Phil's shoulder.

"Uh-oh," said Joe, looking down at the tracks in the dirt. "Frank, you better not come any closer!"

"What are you talking about?" said Frank, going right for his brother.

"What are they?" Phil asked Joe.

But it wasn't Joe who answered him.

Frank stared at the tracks in the dirt—rounder, fatter versions of the squirrel tracks they'd seen earlier. But these tracks were about ten times the size of the squirrel's. Where had he seen those before?

That was when he remembered—the documentary! "B-b-b-bear tracks!"

Chapter
9

DON'T FEED THE ANIMALS

"I got the picture—let's get out of here!" yelled Phil.

They all turned to leave, except Frank Hardy.

"Frank, are you crazy?" Joe asked. "You were the one who was so afraid of the bears! Let's go!"

Frank's heart was pounding—but not for the reason it was earlier, when he'd first gotten off the school bus. Not only did he have to solve a case so soon, but he felt like they were super close to figuring it out!

"C'mon, Frank!" Lolly urged, tugging the cuff of his jacket sleeve.

"Can we please get out of here?" Phil asked. "In case you didn't notice, we're about to be bear stew!"

"I don't think we're in any danger," Frank said. He hoped not, anyway. But it didn't stop his heart from pounding, or his hands from shaking.

Frank looked at his brother, who was now looking at the bear tracks. Joe met his eyes and nodded.

"You see what I see, don't you?" Frank asked.

Joe nodded. "The tracks are going the wrong way."

Lolly sighed. "What are you two talking about?" she asked. "And why aren't we moving?"

"The tracks aren't leading deeper into the woods, the way they should be," Frank explained.

"Where are they leading?" Phil asked, looking horror-struck.

"That's what I plan to find out!" Frank said.

With Frank leading the way, the whole team began to follow the bear tracks—very carefully. They walked off the path, through the thicket of trees and over fallen branches and logs. The sun streamed through the treetops, shining its light on the trail like a flashlight.

"We'd better not get lost!" Lolly said. "Ranger Bo said not to go off the path."

"We're not lost," said Joe. "It's kind of hard to see the tracks, though." He pointed up ahead in the distance, to a big maple tree with polished-looking reddish-purple leaves. "I remember that tree! See how the one next to it has a big hole at the center of the trunk? I remember thinking it looked like a mouth, yawning."

"Where did we see that before?" Phil asked, scratching his head.

Suddenly Frank gasped. "It's where we found our first clue—the feather!"

Lolly drew her eyebrows together in thought. "But that tree was behind the—"

"The tracks are leading right to the visitors' cabin!" Joe finished for her.

"No way!" said Phil. His eyes grew wide.

"I don't like this," Lolly said, her voice wobbling.

"Oh no!" Frank said. "We've got to get back there

and make sure our classmates aren't in danger!"

Joe leaned toward his brother and spoke in a low voice, so only Frank could hear. "But aren't you afraid?"

Frank tilted his chin up. "I'm still afraid. But we have to help the others."

Behind the group, a sound echoed through the woods—the sound of a twig snapping, then another.

Someone was gaining on them! Or some*thing* . . .

"Run!" Joe shouted, hooking his brother's elbow with his own.

Now that the noise was behind them, they ran toward the cabin. Even though it wasn't that far, it felt like forever!

Frank and Joe led the pack, vaulting over a fallen tree limb, then ducking beneath a low-hanging canopy of vines and leaves.

"Don't look back!" Frank told his team as footsteps pounded behind them. "It will only slow us down!"

Thud, thud, thud.

Phil gasped for air. "I don't think I can run anymore!"

"Yes, you can!" shouted Lolly. She grabbed his hand and pulled him forward, alongside her.

"I see the cabin up ahead!" said Joe. "Just a little bit farther!"

As they ran they began to see something yellow that had not been there earlier just off the path. At first it looked like it might be a patch of yellow dandelions, or some kind of wildflower blooming in time for spring.

When they were closer, they saw it was ripped-up pieces of paper from the stolen piñata!

"More piñata pieces!" Joe told Frank. "The paper trail is leading back out to the woods!"

There was a low sound coming from behind them—a deep, rumbling roar.

"Was that a growl?" Phil asked as he ran, the fear plain in his voice.

Frank could almost reach out and touch the back doorknob of the visitors' cabin—they were so close!

The rumble sounded once again, this time louder. *Grrrrr. Grrrrrr!*

"I heard it too!" said Lolly.

"Everyone get inside," Frank said, finally grabbing the doorknob and yanking it open. "Quick!"

"Are you guys okay?" asked Ranger Bo from inside the cabin.

"Shut the door, quick!" Frank told him. "Bear!"

Ranger Bo pulled the door shut once Joe, Frank, Lolly, and Phil were all inside, safe. He peered out the window, the silver in his hair catching a glint in the sunlight.

"Where did you see a bear?" he asked. The usually cheerful look on his face had turned serious.

"We didn't see it," said Joe, "but we heard it!"

On cue, the rumbling started back up outside.

"There it is again!" Frank said.

"That?" Ranger Bo said.

Frank and Joe nodded. To their surprise, Ranger Bo started laughing a big, bearlike belly laugh.

Frank narrowed his eyes. This was no laughing matter!

"I'm sorry, kids," said Ranger Bo. "What you heard isn't a bear."

"It's not?" asked Lolly.

"Then what is it?" Joe asked, crossing his arms.

"See for yourself," Ranger Bo said. He opened the door, and right away, Frank heard the rumbling get louder.

A small machine, about half the size of a car, moved across the grass slowly. There was a man behind the wheel.

"A lawn mower?" Frank asked, embarrassed.

Ranger Bo nodded.

"But something was with us in the woods," argued Lolly. "It was following us!"

"Oh, that?" said a voice in the cabin.

When Frank turned, he saw Adam Ackerman—looking very proud of himself. He smiled. "That was me."

"You chased us?" Frank said angrily. "Why?"

Adam shrugged. "You always think you're better than everyone else. With your stupid mystery club and your dumb notebook. I just wanted to prove that you aren't as brave as you think you are!"

Frank's face burned. He *had* been pretty afraid; Adam was right about that.

"You're wrong," said Lolly, taking a step toward Adam. "Frank is brave."

Frank looked at her, confused. "What do you mean?" he asked. "As soon as we heard those noises in the woods, I ran!"

"Yeah," Lolly said. "But even though you were afraid of the bear, you still followed the tracks to the cabin. You did it to make sure everyone was safe! That's brave."

Ranger Bo stared. "Tracks?" he asked. But no one was paying attention.

Adam sniffed. "Whatever. You still didn't solve your stupid case."

Frank and Joe grinned at each other.

"Do you want to tell him?" Joe asked. "Or should I?"

"I'll get this one," Frank said, pulling his notebook out of his pants pocket and opening it up. "According to my 'stupid notebook,'" he said, "we *did* solve the case."

"Oh yeah?" said Adam, looking doubtful. "Then who did it?"

"No one." Frank smiled. "At least, no one here."

THE HARDY BOYS—and
YOU!

CAN YOU SOLVE THE MYSTERY OF THE MISSING PIÑATA?

Grab a piece of paper and write your answers down.
Or just turn the page to find out.

1. Frank and Joe came up with a list of suspects. Can you think of more? List your suspects.

2. How do you think the piñata disappeared from the cabin? Using the "proof" the boys have so far, write your ideas down!

3. What clues helped you to solve the mystery? Write them down!

Chapter 10

THE BEAR TRUTH

"It was . . . a bear!" Frank said.

Ranger Bo chuckled, patting his chest as he did. "You boys are so funny. What a great joke!"

"You *are* kidding, aren't you?" asked Phil.

Frank shook his head. "When we were looking for animal tracks, we found bear tracks. But they were going *toward* the cabin!"

"And once we got closer to the cabin," Joe said,

"we found shredded bits of the piñata all over the ground, leading back out to the woods."

"Just like the pieces we found out by the tree when we found Heather trying to get better phone service," Frank added.

Ranger Bo frowned. "She is supposed to be helping out—she is on that phone way too much."

Proof! Frank thought, remembering what his dad had told him earlier that morning. He was glad they hadn't gone around accusing all the wrong people of stealing, now that he knew who had really done it. He knew his dad would be proud of him and Joe.

Ranger Bo's mouth dropped open. "But—that's—how—?"

"You said yourself not to feed the animals, right?" said Frank.

"Well, yes," he said.

Frank pointed to the back door. "When we asked Lolly if she'd seen anyone in the cabin earlier—just before the piñata went missing—she said that she was here alone."

"She also said that the back door was open," added Joe.

Ranger Bo put his head in his hands. "Oh no!" he said.

"What's wrong?" asked Lolly.

"I left the door open!" He shook his head. "I can't believe I did that! I'm just so forgetful!"

Frank and Joe remembered earlier in the day, when Ranger Bo had walked away looking for his hat—and it had been right on his head!

"The bear must have been attracted to the candy!" Ranger Bo said. "You boys are right; the bear stole your prize candy!"

"The bear ate all that candy," Lolly said, looking impressed.

"And the toys, too, probably," added Phil.

Just then Heather walked through the front door of the cabin. And in her arms was a great big chocolate-brown piñata—in the shape of a bear!

"I finished filling it with the new candy and toys, Dad," she announced, setting it on the table. "Do we have a winner yet?"

The other teams had been trickling in slowly while Frank and Joe were talking to Ranger Bo. Now they all ran over to examine the new scavenger hunt prize.

Ranger Bo gathered everyone in a circle. He asked them all to pull out their bags of collected clues.

Ellie Freeman's team had found all but the last set of tracks, and Elisa's team had collected every single item, but their Y-shaped twig had broken during the hunt, so it wasn't Y-shaped anymore.

Adam's team and Frank and Joe's team had both collected all the items from the clues, but only one of them had taken pictures of two sets of animal tracks. Squirrel *and* bear tracks!

Ranger Bo beamed down at Frank and Joe Hardy. "Congratulations, kids! It looks like your team gets the piñata!"

Lolly was smiling so wide, it looked like her face would crack! And Phil and Frank were already talking about which toys they hoped would be inside.

Once Heather had hung the piñata up in the middle of the room, she handed Frank a plastic baseball bat. "You think you can break it open?" she asked him.

Frank looked at his team. "Does anyone else want to take the first swing?" he asked.

"You should do it," Lolly said. "You solved the mystery, *and* you were brave."

Frank tightened his grip on the baseball bat while Heather blindfolded him.

Joe and Phil spun Frank in a circle—once, twice, three times.

"Are you ready?" Ranger Bo asked.

"I think so," said Frank.

He tried to retrace his steps to where he thought the piñata was. Then he swung the bat!

On his first try, and his second, the bat didn't even hit the piñata. But on the third try, he heard it connect with a soft thunk.

The group cheered behind him.

Next, Phil and Joe both got a turn. Phil didn't even hit the piñata once, but Joe hit it twice! Still, it hadn't broken open.

It was Lolly's turn.

Once she was blindfolded and spun around three times, she gripped the bat and smiled. Then she took four small steps and swung the bat as hard as she could.

She felt the bat connect to the piñata and, all at once, heard the rush of toys and candy spilling out of it, onto the floor!

• • •

Frank and Joe Hardy were surrounded by a mountain of toys and prize candy.

They were sitting in the secret tree house that their dad had built for them in the Hardys' backyard. Joining them were Phil and the latest member of their mystery-solving club—Lolly Sugarman.

"Ughhhh," Joe groaned. "If I eat one more piece of candy, I'm going to puke!"

Lolly popped a strawberry SugarPop lollipop into her mouth and shook her head. "You shouldn't have tried to eat as much as me," she told him, patting his shoulder. "It takes practice to eat as much as I do—at least, that's what my mom tells me."

Phil and Frank were working together on a cube-shaped puzzle with lots of colors.

"I can't move," Joe complained, slumping in his chair.

Frank laughed. "But everything was deeee-licious!"

"Looks like the Hardy boys have solved another mystery," said Phil.

"I'm proud of you, Frank," said Joe. "Not only did we solve the case today, but you faced a really big fear!"

"And lived to tell the tale." Lolly grinned through her lollipop.

"*You* weren't afraid?" Frank asked Joe. "Not even once?"

"Nope!" Joe placed his hands behind his head. "I guess I'm just not ever afraid."

Frank paused, turning to look out the window of the tree house. "Did you guys hear that?"

"What?" Joe asked, sitting up.

"That growling," said Frank. "*Shhhh* . . . I think it's a . . . BEAR ATTACK!" He turned toward his brother and ran at him with his hands up in the air like claws.

"*Ahhhh!*" Joe screamed.

Frank, Lolly, and Phil doubled over, laughing.

"Our hero," said Frank. "Nothing can scare him!"

"Except my own brother," Joe admitted, joining in the laughter. "And maybe Aunt Gertrude when she tells me to clean my room."

"I think I could get used to being a part of this club," Lolly said, grinning.

Another case solved!

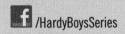

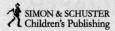